IN ARCTIC WATERS

BY LAURA CRAWFORD
ILLUSTRATION BY BEN HODSON

W9-AZI-159

Thanks to Kate M. Wynne, Marine Mammal Specialist at the University of Alaska Sea Grant Marine Advisory Program, and to Riley Woodford and Sue Steinacher of the Alaska Dept. of Fish and Game, Division of Wildlife Conservation, for verifying the accuracy of the information contained in the "For Creative Minds" section.

Publisher's Cataloging-In-Publication Data

Crawford, Laura.
In arctic waters / by Laura Crawford ; illustration by Ben Hodson.
p. : col. ill. ; cm.
Summary: An arctic adaptation of "This is the house that Jack built" follows polar bears, walruses, seals, narwhals and beluga whales as they chase each other around the ice that floats in the arctic waters. Includes "For Creative Minds" section.
Interest age level: 003-007.
Interest grade level: P-2.
ISBN: 978-0-9768823-4-3 (hardcover)
ISBN: 978-1-934359-34-1 (pbk.)

1. Animals--Arctic regions--Juvenile fiction. 2. Arctic regions--Juvenile fiction. 3. Animals--Arctic regions--Fiction.
4. Arctic regions--Fiction. 5. Stories in rhyme. I. Hodson, Ben. II. Title.

PZ10.3.C73 In 2007[E]   2006924847

Printed in China

Sylvan Dell Publishing
976 Houston Northcutt Blvd., Suite 3
Mt. Pleasant, SC 29464

This is the ice that floats
in the Arctic waters.

This is the fish, small and quick
that circles the ice that floats in the Arctic waters.

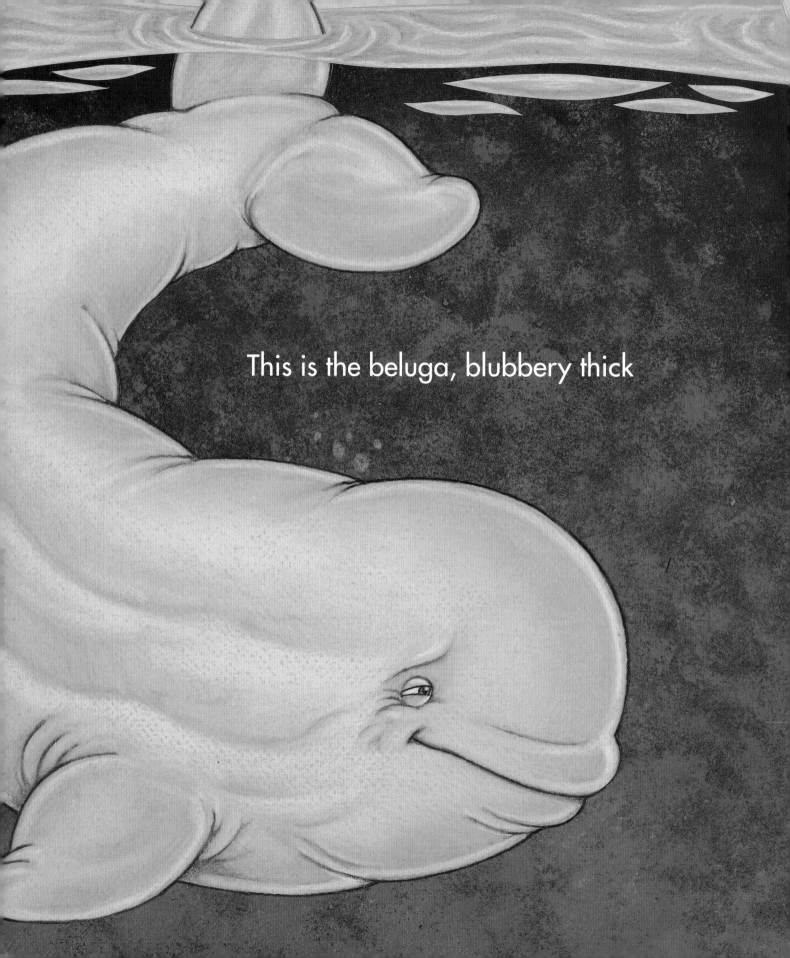

This is the beluga, blubbery thick

that chases the fish, small and quick
that circles the ice that floats in the Arctic waters.

This is the narwhal, big and strong
that swims with the beluga, blubbery thick
that chases the fish, small and quick
that circles the ice that floats in the Arctic waters.

This is the seal, bouncing along
that teases the narwhal, big and strong
that swims with the beluga, blubbery thick
that chases the fish, small and quick
that circles the ice that floats in the Arctic waters.

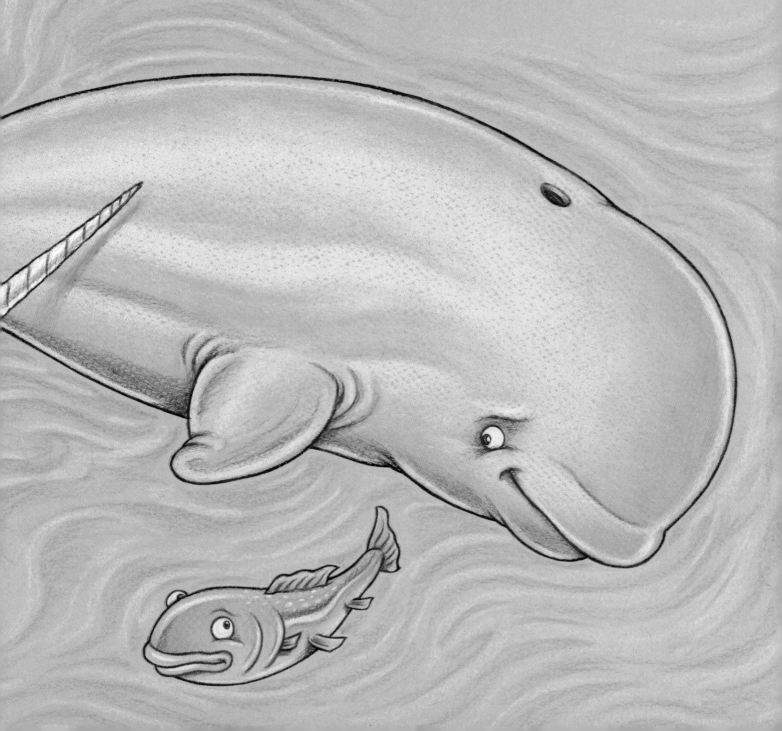

This is the walrus, ready to play
that splashes the seal, bouncing along
that teases the narwhal, big and strong
that swims with the beluga, blubbery thick
that chases the fish, small and quick
that circles the ice that floats in the Arctic waters.

This is the polar bear, furry white
that swats at the walrus, ready to fight
that splashes the seal, bouncing along
that teases the narwhal, big and strong

that swims with the beluga, blubbery thick
that chases the fish, small and quick
that circles the ice that floats in the Arctic waters.

This is the man that hunts the animals
that live on the ice that floats in the Arctic waters . . .

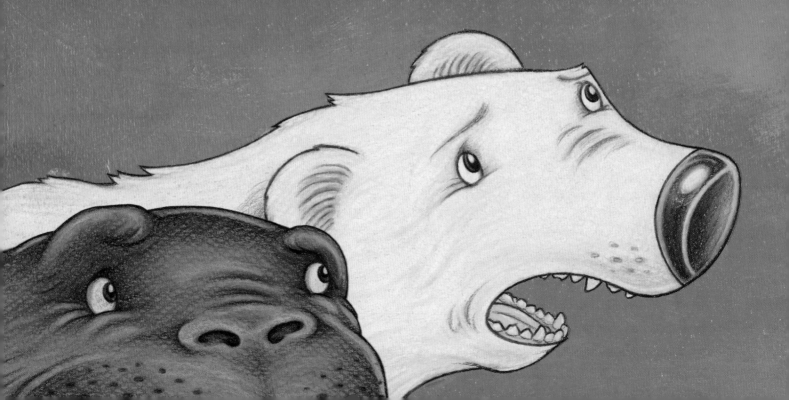

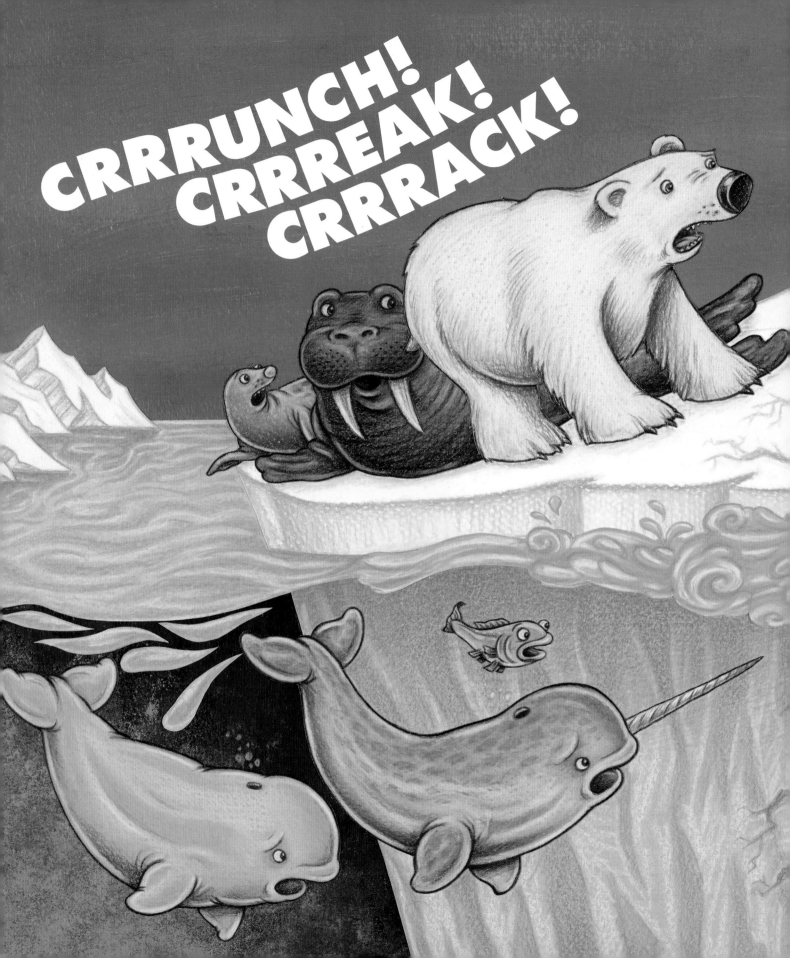

The polar bear stopped . . .

The walrus hopped . . .

The seal scurried . . .

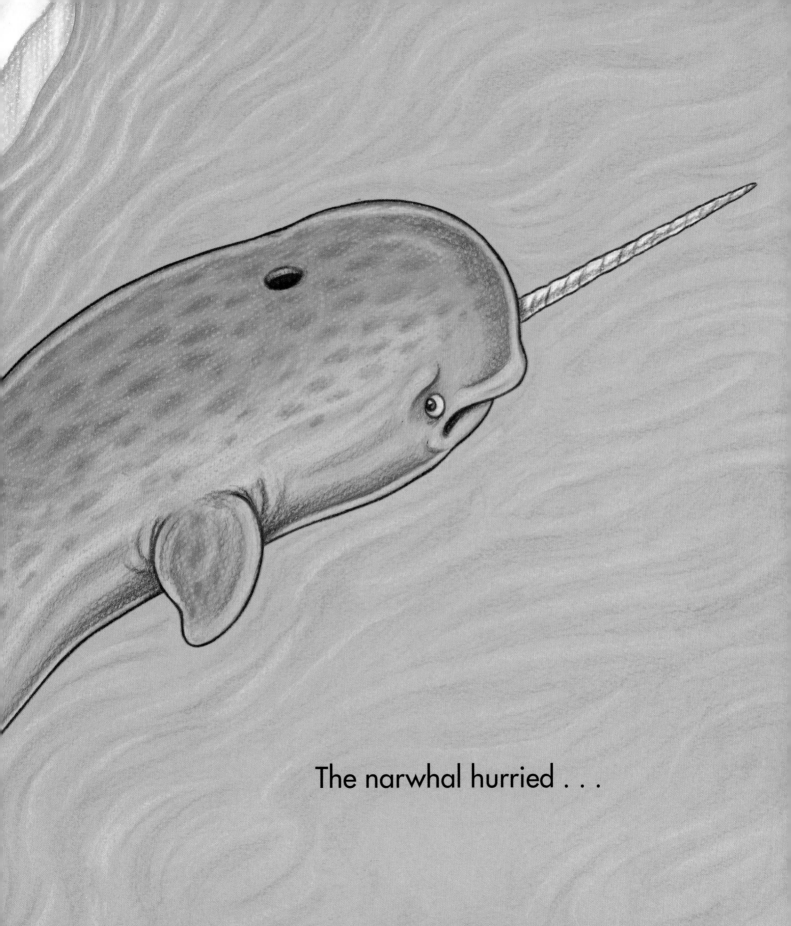

The narwhal hurried . . .

The beluga splashed . . .

The fish dashed . . .

. . . toward a new piece of ice . . .

. . . that floats in the Arctic waters.

For Creative Minds

Arctic Waters

Look at the top part of a globe or a map to see where the Arctic Circle is located. It is north of the 66.5° line of latitude. Everything north of this is referred to as "Arctic" whether it is land or water.

The polar ice cap is one huge mass of the ice that stays frozen all year long–even in the summer.

The summer ice pack stays frozen all year round, but breaks up into smaller ice floes in summer. It floats around the polar ice cap and northern land masses.

The winter ice pack only freezes in winter and thaws each summer. It reaches the coastline of even more northern lands.

The top layer of soil on land in the Arctic generally thaws in the summer and allows plants to grow.

Permafrost is a deeper layer of soil that is always frozen. In some places it has been frozen for thousands of years.

The Inuit

The Inuit are the Natives who live in Canada's coastal Arctic. Inuit means "The Real People." In Alaska and Russia there are several different Native groups that refer to themselves as "Eskimo," but each group has a name in their own language that also means "The Real People." In some areas of the Arctic, the term "Eskimo" is considered insulting. All of these different Native groups hunt marine mammals as an important part of their diet and cultural tradition.

Arctic Animal Adaptations

Animals have special adaptations or behaviors to help them live in the very cold.

They have thick, heavy fur or blubber (a layer of fat) to keep them warm. *What do you do to keep warm in cold weather?*

Many animals also have fur on their wide feet to help them walk on the snow. *Humans sometimes wear snowshoes to help them walk on the snow.*

Sometimes animals hibernate or sleep during the cold winters.

Other animals migrate or go south to warmer weather in the winter.

Polar Bears:
Mammals, carnivores

Polar bears have thick white, water-repellent fur to help them hide in their snowy surroundings and to stay warm in the water.

They even have fur on the bottom of their large feet. Their feet are also very wide to help them them walk on the snow and swim.

Some people say that they have seen polar bears cover their black noses with their white paws to help them hide!

They love to eat seal blubber.

They also eat walruses, narwhals, and beluga whales when they can catch them.

Native hunters and orca whales hunt polar bears.

Other threats to polar bears come from oil drilling, the shrinking of the ice pack that they need to survive, and pollutants in their food.

Polar bear cubs are usually born in dens on land or ice in December.

A mother usually has two cubs at a time.

Cubs live with their mother for about two years and then go off on their own.

Walruses:
Mammals, carnivores

Walruses use their tusks to fight and to help haul themselves up onto ice and land.

The tusks are big teeth.

Both males and females have the tusks but the males' tusks are larger.

The bigger the tusk, the more dominant the walrus is.

Their favorite food is clams. They also eat snails or worms.

They can dive up to 300 feet to get their dinner.

Their biggest predators are orca whales and Native hunters.

Natives eat all parts of the walrus, make drums from the walrus stomach, and use the hide to cover their skin boats, called umiaqs.

The babies are usually born in April or May and can weigh 100 pounds. *How much do you weigh? Is it more or less than a baby walrus?*

Babies stay with their mother about two years.

We can tell how old walruses are by counting the rings in their teeth, just like trees!

Male walruses have air sacs in their necks to keep their heads out of water while they sleep and to make sounds.

They can use all four flippers on land.

They use their extra-sensitive "whiskers" to touch and feel.

Seals
Mammals, carnivores

Several different types of seals live in the Arctic: ringed, bearded, spotted, harp, ribbon, and hooded seals.

Seals in the Arctic are also called "ice seals," because some part of their life cycle happens along the ice pack. Shrinking of the ice pack is a serious threat to seals.

Seals like to eat fish, clams, crabs, squid, and octopus.

Polar bears, orcas, and Native hunters are their biggest predators.

The Inuit and Alaska Eskimos use the meat and blubber for food, and make the hides into rope, boots (called *mukluks*), slippers and many other things.

Narwhal
Mammals, carnivores

The narwhal is not seen very often.

It is called a "unicorn" whale because it has one, very long tooth.

The long tooth grows outward in a spiral and can grow to be 7 to 10 feet long. *Use a yard stick or measuring tape to measure 7 feet. How tall are you? Are you as tall as the tooth of a narwhal?*

Narwhals eat fish, squid, and shrimp.

Their predators are orcas and Inuit hunters. The Inuit eat the meat and blubber and use the skins, oil, and tusks.

Narwhals usually stay close to the ice.

Narwhal calves are usually born in July.

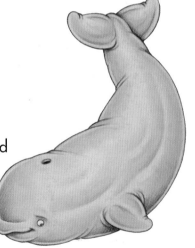

Beluga Whales
Mammals, carnivores

Belugas are medium sized white whales with teeth.

Belugas molt their skin in the summer (July) by rubbing on gravel in shallow water.

Belugas eat a wide variety of fish, shrimp, and squid.

Their predators are polar bears, orcas, and Native Hunters.

Sometimes they get caught in fishing nets.

They migrate in the winter–but do not go farther south than Canada and Alaska.

Baby belugas are born in the summer (May to July) and are about 4.5 feet long. *How tall are you? Are you shorter or taller than a baby beluga?*

Adult belugas range in size from 10 to 15 feet; males are larger than females. *Use a measuring tape to measure 10 and 15 feet.*

Creative Sparks: Mix-and-Match Activity Book

On the next page you will find a template for a mix-and-match book. Photocopy or download the page. Cut out each rectangle containing an animal, then cut along the dotted line just up to the solid gray line (spine). Staple the pages together along the spine. Now you can color and mix and match your animals!

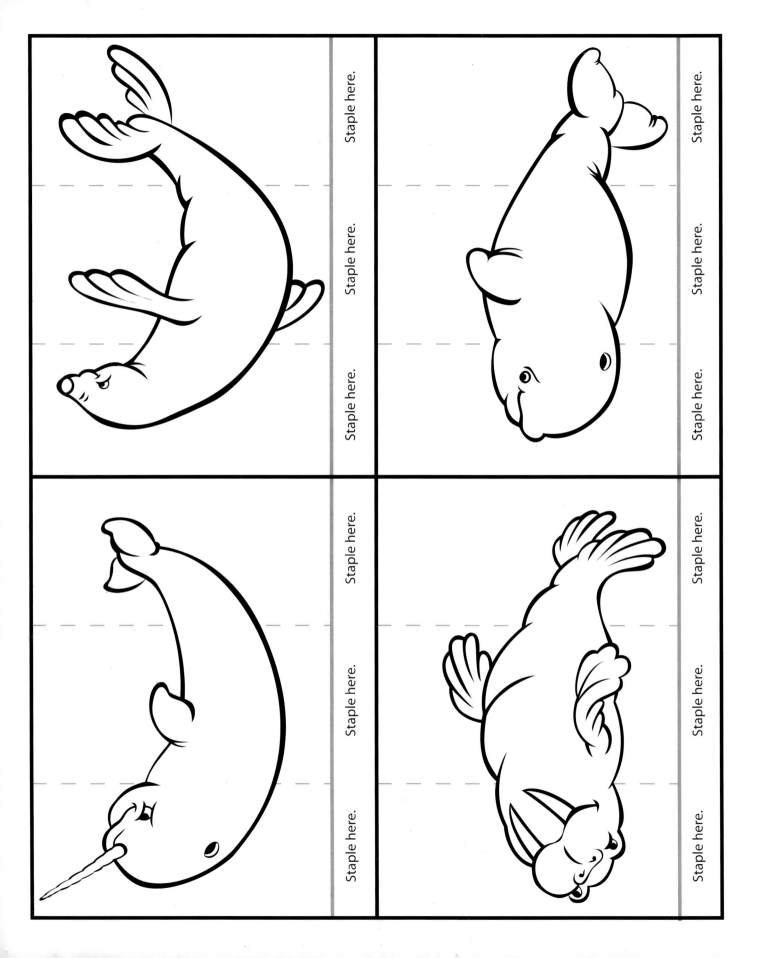